A
Peach Street
Mudders
Story

Stranger in Right Field

by Matt Christopher

Illustrated by Bert Dodson

Little, Brown and Company
Boston New York London

To Paul Michael

First Paperback Edition

The characters and events portrayed in this book are fictitious.
Any similarity to real persons, living or dead, is coincidental
and not intended by the author.

Library of Congress Cataloging-in-Publication Data

Christopher, Matt
    Stranger in right field : a Peach Street Mudders story / by
Matt Christopher.—1st ed.
        p.   cm.
Summary: Who is the new player on the Peach Street
Mudders, and how can Alfie Maples help him improve his
game?
    hc : 0-316-14111-9
    pb : 0-316-10677-1
    [1.Baseball—Fiction.   2. Friendship—Fiction.]   I. Title.
PZ7.C458St   1997
[Fic]—dc21   96-49014

                    hc : 10 9 8 7 6 5 4 3
                    pb : 10 9 8 7 6 5 4 3 2 1

                        hc : WOR
                        pb : COM-MO

PRINTED IN THE UNITED STATES OF AMERICA

1

"Okay!" Coach Parker's voice snapped. "Let's have some quiet!"

The commanding voice struck like a thunderbolt. Silence fell in the Peach Street Mudders' dugout.

"There's someone here I'd like you to meet. Boys, this is Roberti Frantelli."

"Hi!" all fourteen Mudders called out.

The tall, dark-haired boy smiled.

"Thank you. I am happy to be here." He spoke with a strong accent.

Italian? Mexican? Greek? Alfie Maples wondered. He was curious about different countries and cultures. Alfie also wondered why Roberti was dressed in a Peach Street Mudders uniform, as if he were going to play in the game against the Stockade Bulls. He waited eagerly for Coach Parker to explain more about the stranger.

But the coach just said, "Roberti is going to warm up with you outfielders. So let's get out there and show him how the game is played!"

An outfielder? I hope it's not right field! Alfie thought. Ever since he'd joined the team, Alfie had been the starting right fielder. But he knew he wasn't the best player on the team. He sometimes missed easy catches, and he didn't do too well at the plate, either. Still, he hustled during practices and always tried to learn from his mistakes.

Alfie adjusted his glasses and jogged out onto the field. As he passed the bleachers, he spotted a strange-looking man. Unlike most of the fans who were dressed in shorts,

T-shirts, and sunglasses, this man wore a business suit. When the rest of the fans rose to their feet to cheer for the Mudders, he stayed seated.

Even without his glasses, Alfie would have picked the man out of the crowd. The man raised a hand and waved at someone on the field. Alfie turned in time to see Roberti wave back.

"Hey, Alfie, look alive!"

The shout from José Mendez made Alfie snap back to attention. He waved his glove in the air to signal he was ready to catch.

"Roberti, back up so we can throw to you, too," José called. "We'll go around from me to you to Alfie to Barry. Then we'll mix it up. Okay, guys?"

The ball started around slowly. At first, all the boys, including Roberti, made clean catches. Then, at a signal from José, the exercise became more difficult. The ball was thrown high or at the ground on purpose,

forcing the catcher to jump or run in low to retrieve it. Since they weren't throwing in a circle any more, each player had to be ready to catch at all times.

Alfie watched Roberti carefully. To his surprise, the newcomer couldn't seem to get his glove on the ball. By the time Coach Parker called them in for the start of the game, Roberti Frantelli was red-faced from having chased the ball over and over—and the other outfielders were giving him puzzled glances.

Why did the coach let him *on the team?* the looks seemed to ask.

Alfie felt a little sorry for Roberti. But he also felt relieved. After all, he'd worked hard to earn his position as starting right fielder. Seeing Roberti play made him feel he would be able to keep that position, no problem.

2

The game against the Stockade Bulls started a few minutes later.

"We're up first," Coach Parker told the Mudders. "Regular batting order and starting positions as usual, fellas. And I want to hear some chatter from this dugout!"

As the boys gave a cheer, Coach Parker called Alfie and Roberti over to him. He said, "Alfie, as a favor to me, I'd like you to keep an eye on Roberti. Make sure he understands everything that's going on out there. Kind of coach him through the game. Okay?"

Alfie was surprised. It was clear that Roberti could barely catch a ball in a simple practice drill. But now the coach seemed to be saying that Roberti didn't even understand about baseball! If the coach thought that, why had he put Roberti on the team in the first place?

Alfie didn't get it, but he nodded to let the coach know he'd help out. At least he might have a chance to ask Roberti a few questions, like where he was from, if he was visiting or moving to town—and who the man in the business suit was.

Coach Parker clapped his hands a few times and trotted out to the third-base coaching position. Alfie sat down next to Roberti as Barry McGee, the "Hit-Away Kid," picked up a bat and headed toward the plate.

"Okay, Barry! Okay, kid!" Alfie yelled. Even though his mind was on the boy beside him, he wanted the Mudders to know that he was rooting for them one hundred percent.

"A long one, Barry!" Nicky Chong called out from the bench.

Barry pulled down on his helmet as he stepped into the batting box. He let a ball and a strike go by him. Then he belted the next pitch. A high fly to center!

Adzie Healy of the Bulls made an easy catch of it, and Barry was out.

"Nice try, Barry," Alfie said as the outfielder returned to the dugout.

"Yes, nice try," Roberti echoed. Barry glanced at both boys, shrugged, then slumped down on the bench.

First baseman Turtleneck Jones was up next. He took two balls and two strikes, then fanned. Trent Farrell, the Bulls' lanky lefthanded pitcher, seemed to have his fastball working well.

But then José walked, and T.V. Adams doubled. A single from Nicky Chong knocked them both in for two runs scored.

As Alfie stepped to the plate, he saw Nicky

10

STRANGER IN RT. FIELD

watching him with a hopeful look that seemed to say, "Drive me home!"

Coach Parker clapped his hands from the third-base coaching box. "Keep it going, Alfie!" he called. "Make it count!"

Alfie took a deep breath and readied himself for the first pitch. Out of the corner of his eye, he saw Roberti lean forward, his elbows on his knees. Alfie could feel the new boy staring at him.

Suddenly Alfie was nervous. A trickle of sweat ran down his back. One thought ran through his head: *How am I supposed to help Roberti get better at baseball when I have trouble playing the game myself sometimes?*

3

"Steee-rike!" boomed the ump as Trent's first pitch blazed by Alfie.

"At least swing for those, Alfie," Bus Mercer muttered from the on-deck circle. "Don't just stand there."

Alfie didn't. But he missed the next pitch by a mile. Strike two.

"Come on, Alfie!" Bus said.

The pitcher fired in another.

"Ball!" boomed the umpire.

Alfie dug his cleats into the dirt. *This next one won't get by me!* he thought fiercely.

But it did. Trent's pitch was waist high and

outside. Alfie cut at it anyway and swished. Strike three.

"Rats! Made the third out *again!*" Alfie heard Bus say. Alfie felt his face turn red. Even though the other boys often let their teammates know when they were disappointed, Alfie tried not to make comments like that himself. They never made him feel any better, and he knew that they could make someone else feel bad.

Roberti was sitting back with his cap pulled low over his eyes. Beneath the brim, his face was as expressionless as a fresh apple.

Bet he wishes the coach had assigned him to someone other than me, Alfie thought dismally as he grabbed his glove and headed to right field. He took up his position and tried to put Roberti out of his mind by starting up the chatter.

"C'mon, Sparrow! Get 'em out—one, two, three!" he called to the Mudders' pitcher. The rest of the team picked up the chatter.

Sparrow faced the first batter, Jim Hance. Jim laced the ball down to short. Bus picked it off and sent it to Turtleneck at first base for an easy out. The second batter flied out. But Ted Jackson drove a sizzler past Sparrow and Bus. He made it to first.

That was it, though. Adzie Healey popped out to end the inning.

Alfie ran in. When he reached the dugout, he hesitated a long moment before sitting beside Roberti.

"Too bad about your hitting," Roberti said. "How many years have you been play-ing baseball?"

Alfie looked quickly at Roberti. Was the question some kind of wisecrack? Was Roberti suggesting that Alfie didn't look as though he'd been playing for very long?

But Roberti's face was curious, not mean.

"I've been playing for two years," Alfie replied. "How about you?"

Roberti gave a small smile. "I have never played before."

Alfie blinked. More than ever, he wanted to ask how Roberti had gotten onto the Mudders' team. But he was afraid his question might offend the newcomer. After all, Alfie himself had never played before he'd joined the Mudders.

But I had to practice a lot with the guys before I played in my first game, he remembered. *I wasn't just handed a uniform.*

They sat silently for a few minutes. Alfie fished around for something to say. "Uh, is that your dad in the stands?" he finally said. "You know, that guy in the suit?"

Roberti laughed. "Oh, no, that is not my father. That man just takes care of me. He is—"

"Alfie!" Coach Parker interrupted. "Inning's over! Grab your glove and get out there!"

The Mudders had been put down in order: first Bus, then Rudy Calhoun, and last of all

Sparrow had walked up to the plate only to walk back again without a hit. The score remained 2–0.

Chet Barker led off for the Bulls. He popped up a sky-reaching fly above home plate.

"Take it, Rudy!" T.V. shouted from third base.

Rudy did.

Then Trent Farrell hit one out to right field. Alfie should have caught it easily. But at the last moment, he lost sight of the ball! It bounced a few feet behind him. He scrambled to pick it up, then heaved it toward second. Luckily, his throw was right on the money. Trent held at first.

Some good example you're showing Roberti, Alfie thought furiously. *You're catching about as good as he was during practice.*

The inning ended a few minutes later with the Bulls held scoreless. Alfie took a seat on the bench. Roberti excused himself to get a

STRANDED IN RIGHT FIELD

drink of water.

A moment later, Alfie felt someone tap him on the shoulder. It was Bus.

"So, what do you think of the new guy?" Bus whispered.

Alfie shrugged. "Okay, I guess. I haven't had a chance to talk to him much."

Bus nodded. "Kind of funny, though, isn't it? How he just showed up out of nowhere wearing a uniform?"

"It's a little weird," Alfie agreed. "Especially since he told me he's never played baseball before. Did you know the coach asked me to help him out?"

Bus laughed. "*You?* Things are getting even weirder! Unless. . ." Bus's voice trailed off.

"Unless what?" Alfie prodded.

"Unless the coach is training Roberti to play in right field. I mean, why else would he have *you* show him anything?"

Alfie stared at the dirt between his shoes. Bus's words stung, but not because of what he said about the coach replacing him with Roberti. No, what hurt was that Bus didn't think anyone could possibly learn anything about baseball from Alfie Maples!

4

"I brought you some water, Alfie." Roberti handed Alfie a paper cup, then sat down beside him.

"Uh, thanks," Alfie said. Bus raised his eyebrows, but didn't say a word. They sat in silence, watching the game.

Barry had made it to first, held up there while Turtleneck struck out, then reached second on a single by José. T.V. Adams was at the plate. Nicky grabbed a bat and hurried to the on-deck circle.

A moment later, T.V. sent a smasher to right field. Barry made it home, José held up at third, and T.V. stood beaming at second. The score now read Mudders 3, Bulls 0.

Alfie took Nicky's place in the circle. From there he watched Nicky pop out to first.

"Hit the ball, Alfie!" Alfie could hear Roberti's voice loud and clear. "That's right, Alfie, keep it rolling!" Coach Parker called.

Alfie didn't hit a home run, but he did connect with the ball for a blooping infield single. He beat the throw to first by a millisecond. Neither José or T.V. risked advancing.

Bus Mercer came to the plate with the bases loaded. But to everyone's surprise, he struck out and ended the inning.

Disappointed, Alfie was tempted to make a comment to Bus when he met him in the dugout. But he didn't. *Bus might not be able to keep his mouth shut,* Alfie thought, *but I can.*

Alfie picked up his glove and saw Roberti gave him a quick smile, then glance at Bus and back at him knowingly. Alfie smiled back, glad he had held his tongue.

As he ran into the outfield, Alfie found himself remembering his first Mudders game. He had been so scared that he was going to mess up. Coach Parker had been helpful, but mostly Alfie had had to muddle through and learn as he played. It would have been nice to know that someone was keeping a special eye on him. Maybe that's what Coach Parker wanted him to do for Roberti.

The rest of the game sped by quickly. Although the Bulls earned a run, in the end, the Mudders took the game, 3–1.

Alfie joined his teammates shaking the Bulls players' hands. Roberti stepped into place behind him.

"Good game, good game," Alfie said as he slapped each hand that passed him. "See you next game, good effort." He could hear Roberti echoing him.

By the time they'd reached the end of the line, Alfie had made a decision.

I may not be the best player out there, he thought, *but the coach must think I know something worth passing on to Roberti. So that's what I'm going to do.*

And what if he ends up replacing you? a little voice inside him whispered suddenly.

Alfie pushed the thought aside. He gathered up his stuff and started toward the parking lot. That's where his mother usually picked him up after games. Sure enough, the familiar blue sedan was waiting for him.

But it was another car that caught his eye. No, not a car—a limousine! Beside the huge automobile stood the strange man in the business suit. Striding toward it was none other than Roberti Frantelli.

"I will see you at practice tomorrow, Alfie!" Roberti waved as he climbed into the backseat. The man in the business suit slipped in after him. Then the car door slammed and the limousine drove away.

Open-mouthed, Alfie watched it go.

"Wow!" a voice beside him said. It was Bus. "Look at the size of that car! Kinda makes you wonder just who that Frantelli kid is, doesn't it?"

Alfie nodded dumbly. He couldn't have been more surprised than if a spaceship had zoomed out of the sky and landed in the parking lot.

"Better watch out, Alfie," Bus warned. "A kid like that could get whatever he wants. Including a starting position in right field!"

5

That night at dinner, Alfie told his parents all about the mysterious new boy.

"Coach Parker asked me to kind of help him along with the team," he added.

"That's quite a compliment," Mr. Maples said.

Alfie chewed thoughtfully. "I guess so. I hope I don't let him down. I—I'm not really the greatest player out there, you know."

Mrs. Maples ruffled his hair and grinned. "The coach wouldn't have picked you if you weren't the right one for the job."

Alfie thought of Bus's comment in the

parking lot. "But what if Roberti gets really good, really fast? Maybe Coach Parker will replace me!"

Mr. Maples frowned. "I'd be surprised if Coach Parker would do something like that."

"You'll have to trust that the coach will be fair," Mrs. Maples added.

Alfie nodded. He wanted to believe his parents. But deep inside, he knew that if he helped Roberti, then lost his starting position, he'd feel awful.

After dinner, Alfie pulled out his favorite stack of geography magazines and started looking through them. Before too long, he was lost in the photographs of other countries. To him, the people in the pictures looked exotic. Their clothes were like costumes, and their houses and schools were completely different from what he was used to seeing every day. Even the trees and plants were strange. Yet he knew that to these people, he and his surroundings would look just as odd.

I wonder if Roberti is from one of these countries, he thought. *Maybe that's why he doesn't know much about baseball. I think I'll ask him at practice tomorrow.*

6

Practice began at ten o'clock sharp the next morning. Roberti was already at the ball field when Alfie showed up. Alfie started toward him, but Bus Mercer beat him to the punch.

"That was some car you rode away in yesterday. Are you a prince or something?"

Roberti laughed and shook his head. But he didn't offer any explanation of why he was being driven around in such a car.

"Okay, boys, let's get to practice," Coach Parker said. "All outfielders, take a position in the field. The rest of you, line up for some batting practice. The goal is to keep your teammates out there from getting bored. Jack Livingston, come with me to the mound and shag incoming throws from the outfield."

Barry McGee, José Mendez, Alfie Maples, and Tootsie Malone, the usual outfield sub, grabbed their gloves. Alfie hesitated a moment, then called out, "Hey, Roberti, come on with me."

Roberti grinned and picked up his brand-new glove. He caught up to Alfie and the others. Barry took up his position in left field, José moved into center, and Tootsie found a spot in between them. Alfie jogged into right field close to José, then motioned for Roberti to stand a little way away from him on the other side.

When they were ready, Coach Parker had Sparrow and Zero Ford take turns throwing easy-to-hit pitches to their teammates. Soon the fly balls were soaring into the outfield one after another.

Alfie tried to explain the outfielders' movements to Roberti with each hit.

Whap! The ball flew high in the sky to left field.

"See how Barry's holding his glove up like that? That puts his glove in position for the catch. It also helps him block out the sun so he doesn't lose sight of the ball. And when he catches it, he squeezes the fingers of the glove together really tightly *and* makes sure his free hand traps it in the pocket."

Thwack!

"Okay, that ball is coming down right between José and Tootsie. One of them should call for it so that the other one backs away. Otherwise, crash! They'll run into each other!"

Pow! Another ball soared way up and behind Barry.

"It's usually better to run backwards to catch a fly ball over your head than to turn around and run. If you turn, you could be off-balance or lose sight of the ball for a second."

But a moment later, when Alfie tried to back up to make a catch, he tripped over his feet and fell. While the other outfielders laughed good-naturedly, he grinned sheepishly. "Well, maybe sometimes it's better to turn around and chase it!" he admitted as Roberti helped him up.

The next ball hit headed between Alfie and Roberti. Alfie hesitated, then called for Roberti to take it.

Roberti did everything just as Alfie had suggested: He held the glove high, backed up a few quick steps, squeezed the fingers together when the ball hit the pocket, then cupped his other hand over it to be sure it was trapped. He fished the ball out triumphantly.

"Okay, just get it as near Jack as you can," Alfie started to say. But he needn't have bothered. With a pinpoint accurate throw, Roberti hurled the ball in. It smacked solidly into Jack's glove.

Roberti grinned at Alfie. "How did I do?"

"That was just right," Alfie said. "You catch on quickly." *Almost too quickly,* he added worriedly to himself. *And what an arm!*

7

The next morning, Alfie woke up to the sound of rain pounding on the window. He knew practice would be cancelled, so he rolled out of bed and padded downstairs in his pajamas. He was just finishing a bowl of cereal when the phone rang. His mother picked it up, then called out that it was for him.

"Hello?"

"Alfie! I hope I am not calling you too early in the morning?" It was Roberti.

Alfie told him he wasn't.

"Oh," said Roberti. "I was thinking to

myself, do you know how to swim?"

"Swim?" Alfie echoed. "Yeah, I know how to swim."

"Good!" Roberti said happily. "Then would you like to go swimming with me today?"

"But it's raining!"

"There is a place we can go where we will not get wet."

Alfie started to laugh. "Okay, but it's going to be pretty tough to stay dry while we're swimming!"

Roberti laughed, too. Alfie ran to ask his mother if it was okay for him to go.

"Let me talk to Roberti's guardian," she said. Alfie relayed the message to Roberti.

A moment later, Mrs. Maples was talking with someone on the other line. Alfie hung around, waiting for her to finish. Suddenly Mrs. Maples glanced at him, then turned around in her chair and continued speaking in a low voice.

Alfie thought that was strange, but forgot

all about it when Mrs. Maples called out that Roberti would be by in fifteen minutes to pick him up.

Alfie raced up the stairs to find his suit and a towel. He packed both into his knapsack, then changed into shorts, a T-shirt, and a sweatshirt before going back downstairs carrying the pack.

As he passed the living room door, he paused, then went in. He pulled a few geography magazines from his pile to take with him. *Maybe I can ask Roberti if he's from one of these places,* he thought.

A little later, the doorbell rang. "Mom, Roberti's here! I'm leaving now!" Alfie called.

"Well, hold on one second. I'd like to meet your new friend." She came around the corner just as Alfie opened the door for Roberti.

"My goodness!" Mrs. Maples exclaimed. For a moment, Alfie didn't know what was wrong. Then he realized that Roberti had been driven over in the limousine. It idled at the curb.

"Mom, this is Roberti. Roberti, this is my mom. Can we go now?"

Roberti smiled at Mrs. Maples and held out his hand. "It is very nice to meet Alfie's mother," he said. "My guardian said you had a nice talk earlier. Are you ready to go swimming, Alfie?"

His mother nodded that it was okay for him to go. Alfie thought he heard her mumble something about "a car big enough to swim in" just as the front door closed.

Awed, Alfie sat down in the huge backseat of the limo. Roberti flopped next to him and pointed to the magazines Alfie held tightly. "What are those?" he asked.

Suddenly Alfie wasn't sure he wanted to show them to Roberti. What if Roberti thought they were dumb?

"Oh, they're just some old magazines," he mumbled. He flipped through the pages of one, then tried to tuck it into his knapsack. But Roberti pulled it out of his hands. His eyes were bright, and he was grinning broadly.

"I have copies of these magazines, too," he said. "I had to leave mine at home. I hope you will let me look through these today!"

"Sure!" Alfie said, relieved. "Here, let me show you my favorite pictures."

For the next fifteen minutes, the two boys turned through the pages of color photographs and illustrations. Alfie was surprised at how familiar Roberti seemed with several of the places pictured.

"Did you live in all these countries?" Alfie finally asked.

Roberti shrugged. "I have traveled to some. Others are places I will someday visit."

"How do you know that?" Alfie wondered.

Roberti smiled but didn't answer. Instead, he pointed out the window. "Here we are, at the swimming place!"

Alfie looked up in amazement. They were parked in front of a fancy hotel located in the next town. Alfie had seen a picture of it in the newspaper once, but he had never dreamed he'd be going inside.

"Wow!" he breathed. "It's like a palace!"

Roberti laughed. "Come on!" he said.

For the next three hours, the boys splashed and played in the hotel's pool. When they got hungry, Roberti asked his guardian to order them some burgers, fries, and thick milkshakes.

While they ate, Roberti surprised Alfie by peppering him with questions about baseball, especially about right field. Alfie shared all he could, often using stories about mistakes he had made to explain the right and wrong way to do things in the field.

"You know how I told you about getting back in time to catch a long fly ball? Well, one time when I first started playing, a high fly ball was going really far behind me. I couldn't make up my mind if I should run backwards or turn around. So I ended up trying to do both at the same time! Coach Parker said I looked like I was caught in a twister." Laughing, he shook his head at the memory.

"It must be fun to play baseball all the time," Roberti said wistfully.

Alfie shrugged. "Well, maybe you can play in a game sometime," he said.

"Yes," Roberti said with a strange smile. "Maybe even very soon."

8

Coach Parker called for a make-up practice the day after the rainstorm.

"We've got a big game against the Dragons coming up!" he reminded everyone when they gathered at the field.

For the first drill, he put his regular infield lineup in position except for the pitcher. Then he told all the outfielders, including the subs, to get into position. The remaining players would act as batters and run the bases after each hit.

As Alfie and Roberti waited in the field together, Alfie tried to explain the rules about where to throw the ball when a runner was on base.

"If the bases are empty, it's easy—the throw goes to first. But if there's a runner on first and the batter gets a base hit, the runner has to move to second, right? So where do you throw?"

Alfie could see Roberti working it out in his head. "Second?" Roberti answered.

"Right! If your throw is good and strong, the ball will beat him there and he'll be out. That's called a force-out. And then if the second baseman can throw the batter out at first, you can turn that into a double play."

Just as he had the day before, Roberti seemed to soak up all the information Alfie was giving him. He asked questions when he didn't understand something.

"But what if the runner is at second base and there is no runner behind him who is forcing him to move? Should I throw to third?"

Alfie thought for a moment. "That's a tricky one. It's bad when a runner gets to third base, because then he's in scoring position. But since he doesn't *have* to run from second to third, you might be in better shape if you throw out the batter at first." Alfie pondered further. "I guess the most important thing is to make a quick decision and a good throw."

Roberti nodded. "A good throw, yes. I will try."

The drill started. One fly ball after another soared into the outfield. One throw followed the next. Sometimes the throw beat the runner, but sometimes the runner was safe. Roberti made a few mistakes, dropped a few balls, and chased a few others, but by the end of the drill, all the outfielders could see that he had improved from the last practice.

When Coach Parker called them in at the end of practice, the outfielders all jogged along together.

José fell in next to Roberti. "Wow! I can't

believe you're the same guy!" he said.

Tootsie nodded. "Yeah, looks like we've got another good outfield sub. Just in time, too, because my folks and I are going on vacation next week. Now I don't have to leave the Mudders short a man!"

"Thank you for your kind words," Roberti said. His face was flushed with happiness. "Alfie is very good to teach me."

Barry laughed. "Yup, ol' Alfie here really knows how to talk the game. In fact, I wonder if the student is going to beat out his teacher soon?"

Roberti looked at Alfie curiously. Alfie reddened. He was glad practice was over for the day so he could ignore Barry's gibe. He just hoped that look from Roberti didn't mean he took the comment seriously.

But as he left the field, something Roberti had said the day before stuck in his mind— something about playing in a baseball game *very soon*.

9

"Hey, Alfie, we're going to get together a pickup game later today. Wanna come?"

Nicky Chong had run to catch up with Alfie in the parking lot. Roberti was with him.

"Please, Alfie, it is important for me to see you play," Roberti said.

Why is that? Alfie wondered suddenly. *So you can see if you're getting better than me?*

He quickly pushed the thought away. *Roberti isn't like that,* he tried to assure himself. He agreed to meet up with everyone after lunch.

"Great, see you then!" Nicky said. He ran

off to nab Turtleneck. Roberti climbed into the back of the waiting limousine, waved to Alfie, and sped off.

Later in the day, they all met again on the field. They chose up teams. Alfie and Roberti were on opposite sides, but both were playing right field.

"I wish we were on the same team, Alfie," Roberti said. "I was hoping you could tell me the best way to get a hit."

Alfie gulped. When he was playing in the outfield, he knew he could mess up from time to time without anybody coming down on him too hard. After all, everybody dropped a few balls or made a few lousy throws now and then. But at the plate it was a different story. There, all eyes were on you. And if you failed to get a hit too many times in a row, people started to talk.

He finally answered the only way he knew how. "Just keep your eye on the ball and swing to meet it. Just remember, I'll be waiting for it!" Alfie punched his fist into his glove and headed out to right field.

When everyone was in position, Roberti trotted to the batter's box and held the bat over his shoulder. Sparrow threw a nice straight pitch.

Wham!

Roberti clubbed the ball in a hard line drive right between first and second. Turtleneck and Nicky were so stunned, they just let it bounce into right field.

"Holy cow!" catcher Rudy Calhoun yelped.

"I did it, Alfie—I kept my eye on the ball and met it!" Roberti cried as he rounded the bases.

Alfie was too busy chasing the ball to answer back. But he couldn't stop his thoughts. *I'll say you did. You're a natural at the plate. A real natural. You sure didn't need me to give you any pointers. I wonder if you ever did....*

The game continued for another hour, then broke up. Roberti had stunned everyone by getting hit after hit and making clean catches and throws most plays. They all crowded around the newcomer in right field, who laughed and joked along with them. Only Alfie hung back. But he didn't miss Roberti whispering to Bus. Bus glanced over at Alfie with a surprised look on his face, then nodded and whispered back.

Alfie slowly gathered up his gear. As he left the dugout, he overheard Roberti talking to Bus.

"That's right," he said. "I will be playing right field very soon."

Alfie felt like Roberti had just punched him in the stomach. And it hurt something fierce.

10

Alfie sat with his chin in his hands, poking at his cereal. His glove lay on the table next to him and he was dressed in his Mudders uniform. But the last thing he felt like doing was playing baseball.

All night long, he had thought about what Roberti had said the day before.

You think a guy is your friend. Then he goes and pulls something like this! Alfie thought miserably.

Alfie's mother came into the kitchen. She glanced at the clock, then at her son.

"Hey, sport, aren't you going to be late for

your game? You're usually calling all over the house for me to come drive you by now!"

Alfie sighed, then picked up his glove. "Okay, I guess it's time to go," he said as he dumped his bowl into the sink and filled it with water.

The car ride to the game was silent until they pulled into the parking lot. Roberti's limousine was already there, but Alfie barely looked at it. He was about to get out of the car when his mother stopped him.

"Alfie, what's wrong?" she asked softly. "I've never seen you so glum right before a game."

Then it all came rushing out: How Alfie had done his best to be Roberti's friend and coach despite his concerns for his own position. And how now it looked like Roberti was going to take over his spot.

"And that's what really hurts, isn't it? You feel like he used you?" Mrs. Maples finished for him. Alfie hung his head and nodded.

"Well, I think we'd better go clear this up. Come on."

Alfie started to protest, but his mother ignored him. She marched right to the dugout.

Most of the team was already gathered there. Roberti was right in the center, laughing and talking with the others as if he had been a Mudder since the squad had started.

"Alfie! There you are!" Roberti broke through the ring of boys and headed toward Alfie. "Guess what! Coach Parker said—"

"Roberti!" Mrs. Maples interrupted. Alfie looked up at her in surprise. "Don't you think you had better wait for Coach Parker to make that announcement, Roberti?" Roberti gave Mrs. Maples a strange smile, then nodded knowingly.

"Yes, perhaps it would be best for him to be here, too," Roberti agreed.

Alfie frowned. *When did Mom and Roberti become so chummy?* he thought. He suddenly became aware that the other boys were whispering, giving him sidelong glances, and trying to hold back laughter. The air was thick with excitement.

Alfie couldn't stand it any longer. "Okay, what's going on?" he asked angrily. "Somebody better tell me what the big secret is or—"

"Or what?" a voice boomed behind him.

Coach Parker strode up to the dugout, followed by Roberti's guardian. "Well, Alfie?"

But it was Roberti who spoke. "Coach Parker, I want to tell Alfie the good news!" he said.

"Don't bother—I already know what it is," Alfie mumbled.

Roberti's eyes widened. "You do?" he asked.

"Well, it doesn't take a rocket scientist to figure out that you're taking over the starting right field position," Alfie replied.

To Alfie's amazement, Roberti started

laughing. The other Mudders joined in, as did Coach Parker, his mother, and Roberti's guardian.

Roberti cried, "Oh, Alfie, I am sorry to be laughing. But it is because I am so happy to tell you that that is not true!"

"Perhaps I can explain." Roberti's guardian stepped forward. He introduced himself as Mr. Bannon. He laid one hand on Alfie's shoulder, the other on Roberti's, and turned the boys so that they were facing each other.

"Alfie, I'd like you to meet Roberto Fernandez." He paused for a moment. "Movie star."

Alfie's jaw dropped. "*A movie star?*" he exclaimed.

Roberti—no, Roberto—grinned. "Well, I have only been in a few films, so I am not a movie *star* yet," he said. "But if the movie I am soon to act in is a success, then perhaps I will be!"

Coach Parker cleared his throat. "I was

sworn to secrecy about Roberto and the movie business. But I bet you can guess what Roberto's movie is about, can't you, Alfie?"

Alfie looked at Roberto, who waggled his glove at him and tipped back his baseball cap.

"Baseball! The movie's going to be about baseball!" Alfie guessed.

"That's right. To be exact, it's the life story of a famous baseball player. Roberto is going to play the main character as a boy," Coach Parker told him.

"I will be in most of the first scenes," Roberto added. Then he glanced up at Mr. Bannon. "Can I tell him now?"

Mr. Bannon nodded.

"I will be in most of the first scenes," Roberto repeated. "And you will be in one!"

Alfie gasped. "*What?*" he squeaked.

"That's right, Alfie," his mother said, beaming. "If you want to be in the movie, your father and I have said it's okay."

"But I don't know how to act!"

"I will teach you," Roberto said. "Just like you taught me about baseball—and about sportsmanship, and about friendship. I would be honored to teach you about the movies if you would let me."

"It's—it's a deal!"

Coach Parker thumped his clipboard. "Well, now that that's settled, do you boys think we can get this game started?" As the Mudders came to attention, Mrs. Maples and Mr. Bannon moved off to the stands. "Here's the lineup: left field, Barry McGee; center field, José Mendez; right field—"

"Roberto Fernandez!" Alfie cried. The other boys laughed as Coach Parker shot Alfie a look. Alfie spread his hands wide and looked innocent. "Hey, I'm not saying I'm giving up my position for all time, but we may never get another chance to play a baseball game *and* see a movie preview at the same time. Besides, Roberto here may still need some more pointers!"

A
Peach Street
Mudders
Story

The action-packed Peach Street Mudders series by Matt Christopher:

All-Star Fever
The Catcher's Mask
Centerfield Ballhawk
The Hit-Away Kid
Man Out at First
Shadow Over Second
The Spy on Third Base
Stranger in Right Field
Zero's Slider

Join the Matt Christopher Fan Club!

To get your official membership card, the Matt Christopher *Sports Pages*, and a handy bookmark, send a business-size (9½" x 4") self-addressed, stamped envelope and $1.00 (in cash or a check payable to Little, Brown and Company) to:

Matt Christopher Fan Club
c/o Little, Brown and Company
3 Center Plaza
Boston, MA 02108